# THE FAT CONTROLLER

### Based on *The Railway Series* by the Rev. W. Awdry

Illustrations by
*Robin Davies*

EGMONT

# EGMONT

*We bring stories to life*

First published in Great Britain in 2007
by Egmont UK Limited
239 Kensington High Street, London W8 6SA
This edition published in 2008
All Rights Reserved

HiT entertainment

ISBN 978 1 4052 3497 9
1 3 5 7 9 10 8 6 4 2
Printed in Italy

The Forest Stewardship Council (FSC) is an international, non-governmental organisation
dedicated to promoting responsible management of the world's forests. FSC operates a
system of forest certification and product labelling that allows consumers to identify
wood and wood-based products from well managed forests.

For more information about Egmont's paper buying policy please visit www.egmont.co.uk/ethicalpublishing

For more information about the FSC please visit their website at www.fsc.uk.org

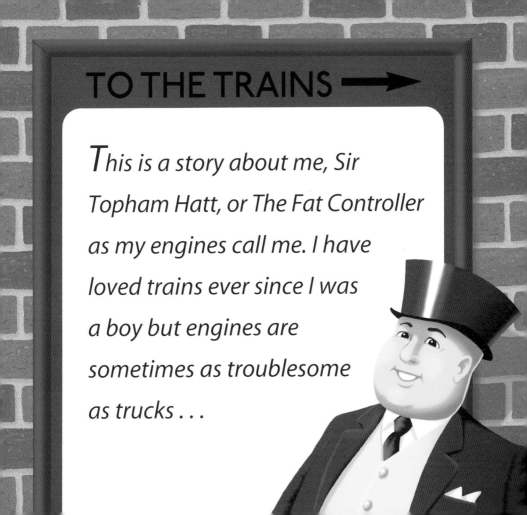

*This is a story about me, Sir Topham Hatt, or The Fat Controller as my engines call me. I have loved trains ever since I was a boy but engines are sometimes as troublesome as trucks . . .*

One morning, The Fat Controller was eating his usual breakfast of toast and marmalade. Lady Hatt was pouring him a cup of coffee, when the telephone rang.

"Bother that telephone!" said The Fat Controller, frowning.

"I'm sorry, my dear," he said to Lady Hatt, a few minutes later. "The engines are not behaving themselves, I must go at once. Engines on my Railway do as they are told!"

When he arrived at the Main Station, there was a tremendous noise. The passengers waiting on the platform were angry.

The Fat Controller went into his office and sat down behind his desk.

Moments later, the Stationmaster knocked on the door. "There's trouble in the shed, Sir," he said. "Henry is sulking. There's no train and the passengers are saying this is a bad Railway."

"Indeed," said The Fat Controller. "We cannot allow that."

At the sheds, The Fat Controller found Gordon, James and Henry looking very cross.

"Come along, Henry. It's time your train was ready," said The Fat Controller, firmly.

"Henry's not going," said Gordon. "We won't shunt like common tank engines. That is Thomas' job."

"We are important tender engines. Fetch our coaches and we will pull them. Tender engines don't shunt!" huffed Henry.

"Oh, indeed," said The Fat Controller. "We'll see about that. Engines on my railway do as they are told."

And he hurried away in his car to find Edward.

"The Yard has never been the same since Thomas left to run his branch line," he thought, sadly. And he took out a handkerchief to mop his brow.

Meanwhile, Edward was shunting.

"Leave those trucks, please, Edward," said The Fat Controller. "I want you to push coaches for me in the Yard."

"Thank you, Sir, that will be a nice change," said Edward, happily.

"That's a good engine, off you go then."

So Edward found coaches for Gordon, James and Henry, and that day the trains ran as usual.

But the next morning, Edward looked unhappy.

Gordon came clanking past, hissing rudely.

"Bless me," said The Fat Controller. "What a noise!"

"They all hiss me, Sir," sighed Edward. "They say tender engines don't shunt and that I have dirty wheels like the trucks. I haven't, have I, Sir?"

"You have nice blue ones, Edward," said The Fat Controller, kindly. "Tender engines do shunt, but we need another tank engine here."

The Fat Controller went to the Workshop and inspected all sorts of engines. At last, he saw a little green tank engine with four wheels.

"That's the one," he thought. The Fat Controller knew a Really Useful Engine when he saw one. "If I choose you, will you work hard?" he said.

"Oh, Sir. Yes, Sir!" peeped the little green engine.

"That's a good engine. I'll call you Percy," smiled The Fat Controller.

And he drove him all the way back to the Yard.

"Edward . . ." he called, "here's Percy. Will you show him what to do?"

Percy soon learned what needed doing, and he and Edward had a happy afternoon.

Then Henry steamed by, hissing as usual.

"Wheeeesh!" little Percy hissed back.

Henry was so surprised, he almost jumped off the track!

The next day, The Fat Controller arrived. Edward, Thomas and Percy were excited.

He told the engines that Henry, Gordon and James were sulking. "They refuse to shunt like 'common tank engines', so I have shut them in the shed. I want you to run the line for a while."

"Common tank engines indeed!" snorted Thomas. "We'll show them."

"And Percy will help, too."

"Thank you, Sir!" whistled Percy, with delight.

Edward and Thomas worked the Main Line, peep-peeping to each other as they passed by.

Percy puffed along the Branch Line, carrying passengers to their stations.

Thomas was worried about Annie and Clarabel, but his Driver and Guard promised to look after them.

There were fewer trains, but the passengers didn't mind. They knew the three naughty engines were being taught a lesson.

In the shed, Gordon, James and Henry were cold, lonely and miserable.

There was no coal for them, no washdown and they missed their passengers.

They wished they hadn't been so silly.

The next morning, The Fat Controller visited the shed. He could see that the engines had learned their lesson.

"We are sorry, Sir," said Gordon.

"We were too big for our buffers!" added James.

"Remember, only Really Useful Engines can work on my railway!" said The Fat Controller. He knew just how to handle difficult engines.

From that moment on, the three tender engines were never rude to tank engines again.

**The Thomas Story Library is THE definitive collection of stories about Thomas and ALL his friends.**

5 more Thomas Story Library titles will be chuffing into your local bookshop in August 2008!

**Jeremy**
**Hector**
**BoCo**
**Billy**
**Whiff**

And there are even more Thomas Story Library books to follow late

**So go on, start your Thomas Story Library NOW!**

## A Fantastic Offer for Thomas the Tank Engine Fans!

STICK POUND COIN HERE

In every Thomas Story Library book like this one, you will find a special token. Collect 6 Thomas tokens and we will send you a brilliant Thomas poster, and a double-sided bedroom door hanger! Simply tape a £1 coin in the space above, and fill out the form overleaf.

**TO BE COMPLETED BY AN ADULT**

To apply for this great offer, ask an adult to complete the coupon below
and send it with a pound coin and 6 tokens, to:
THOMAS OFFERS, PO BOX 715, HORSHAM RH12 5WG

☐ Please send a Thomas poster and door hanger. I enclose 6 tokens
plus a £1 coin. (Price includes P&P)

Fan's name...................................................................................

Address.....................................................................................

.............................................................Postcode.............................

Date of birth...............................................................................

Name of parent/guardian...............................................................

Signature of parent/guardian.........................................................

Please allow 28 days for delivery. Offer is only available while stocks last. We reserve the right to change
the terms of this offer at any time and we offer a 14 day money back guarantee. This does not affect your
statutory rights.

☐ Data Protection Act: If you do not wish to receive other similar offers from us or companies we
recommend, please tick this box. Offers apply to UK only.